SAGINAW CHIPPEWA ACADEMY
LIBRARY MEDIA CENTER
MT. PLEASANT, MI 48858

WITHDRAWN

Buffy's Anger

Doggie Tails Series

Buffy's Anger

Doggie Tails Series

By David M. Sargent, Jr.

Illustrated by Jeane Lirley Huff

Ozark Publishing, Inc.
P.O. Box 228
Prairie Grove, AR 72753

Cataloging-in-Publication Data

Sargent, David M., 1966–
    Buffy's anger / by David M. Sargent, Jr. ; illustrated by Jeane Lirley Huff.—Prairie Grove, AR : Ozark Publishing, c2004.
        p. cm. (Doggie tails series)

    SUMMARY: Emma, the new baby, finally begins to befriend the others—all except Buffy.
        ISBN 1-56763-855-4 (hc)
        ISBN 1-56763-856-2 (pbk)

    [1. Jealousy—Fiction. 2. Dogs—Fiction. 3. Stories in rhyme.] I. Huff, Jeane Lirley, 1946– ill. II. Title. III. Series.

    PZ8.3.S2355Au 2004
        [E]—dc21   200310287

Copyright © 2004 by David M. Sargent, Jr.
All rights reserved

Printed in the United States of America

Inspired by

Buffy's jealousy of the new baby.

Dedicated to

All multiple-dog owners.

Emma came to us
When she was seven weeks old.
The three girls gave her
A shoulder that was cold.

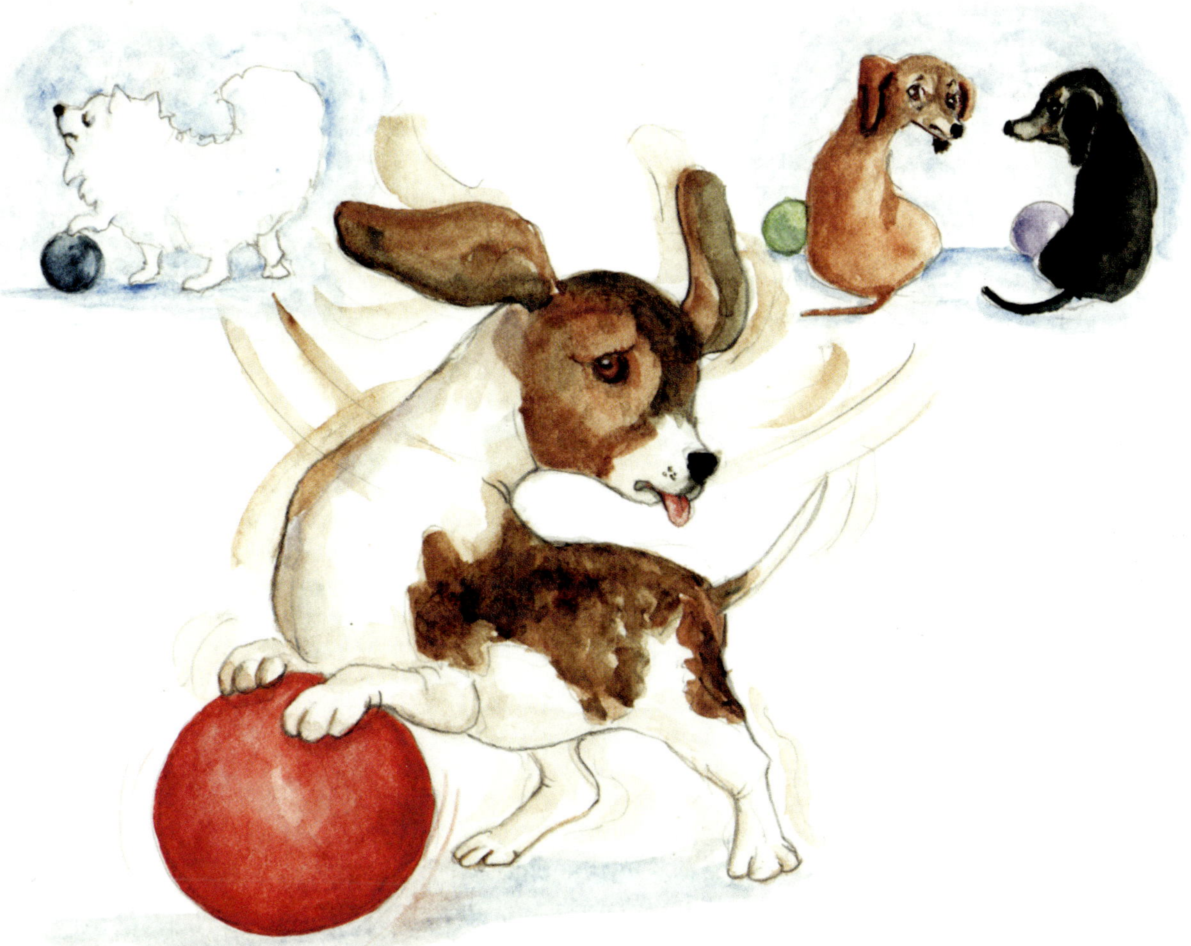

She was really cute
And full of life,
Which filled the others'
Heads with strife.

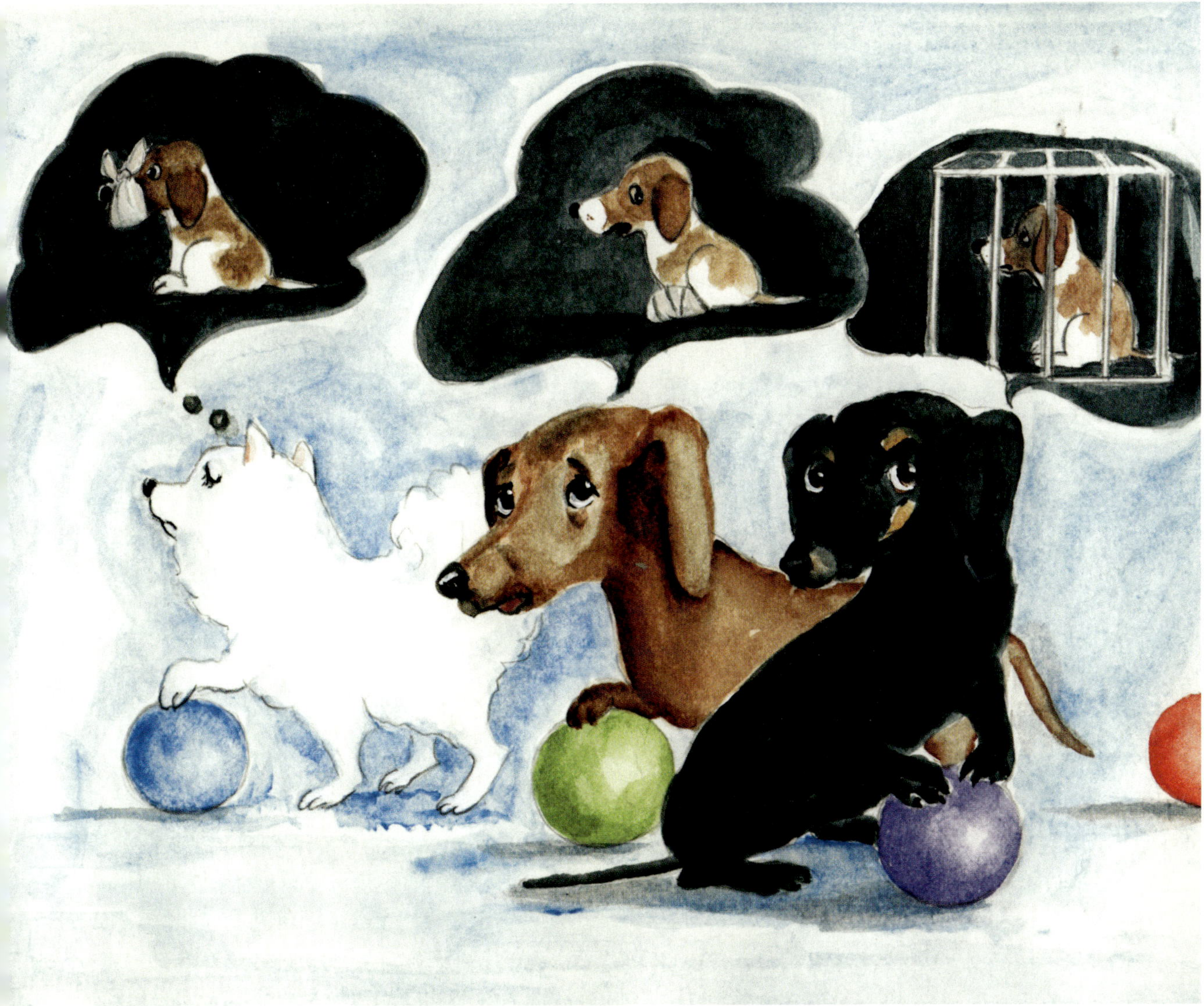

Mary was the first one
To accept her.
I think it was for
The warmth of her fur.

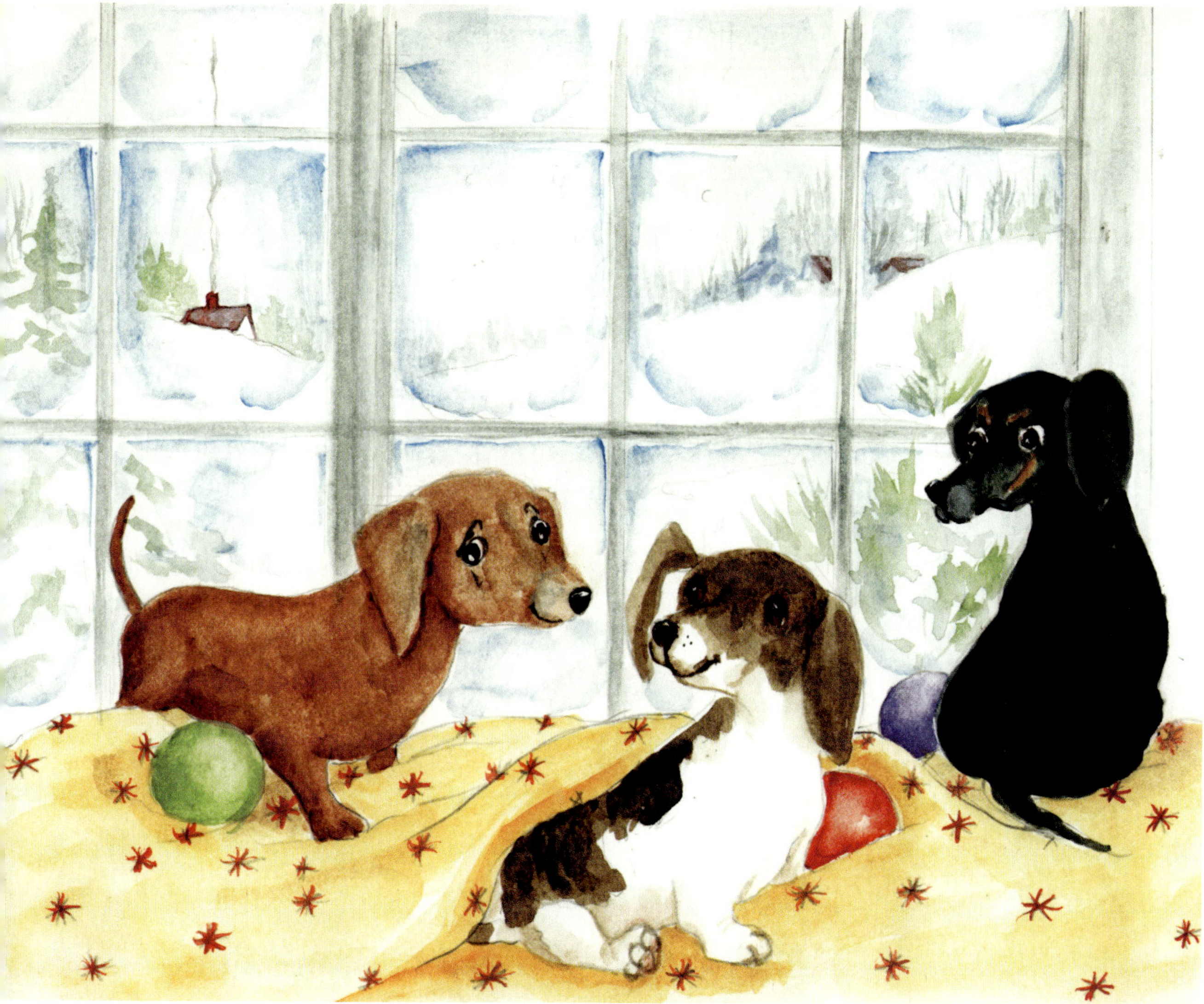

Right next to Emma,
She'd lay down
And keep her company
While I went to town.

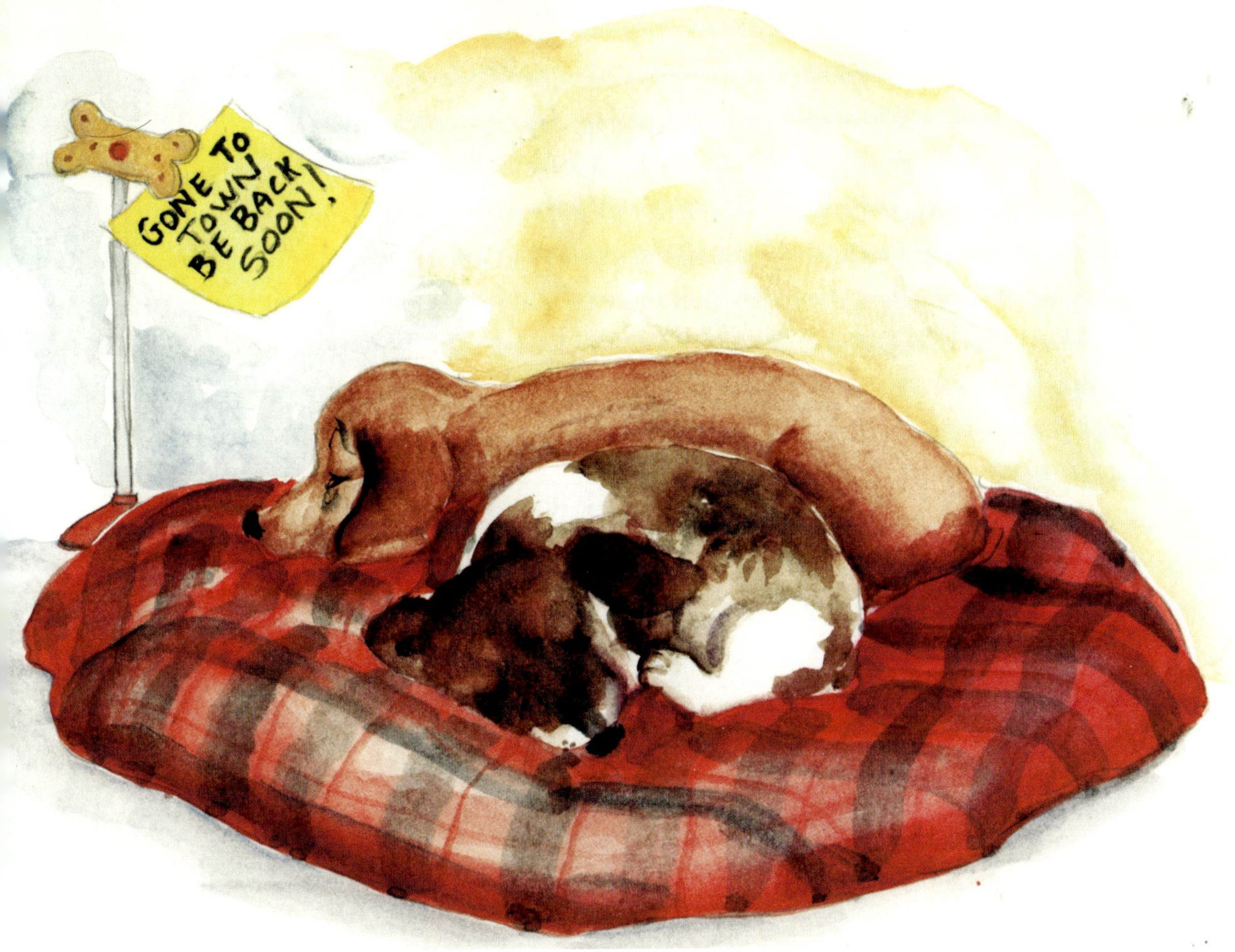
GONE TO TOWN BE BACK SOON!

Emma got her first kiss
While we were in Tennessee.
And I must say,
Mary really surprised me.

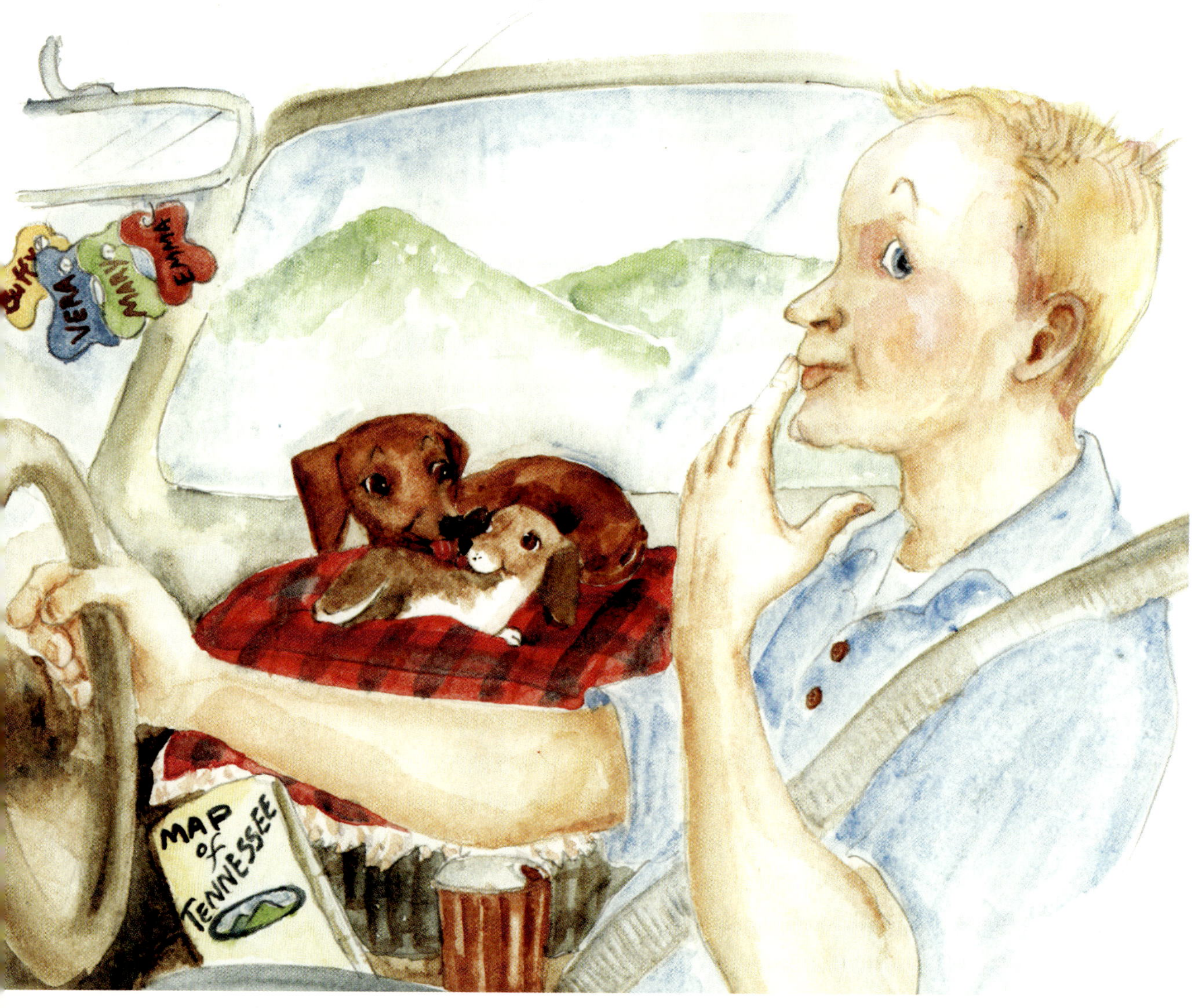
BUFFY
VERA
MARY
EMMA
MAP of TENNESSEE

Vera was the next one
To play with the baby.
And that made me think
That just maybe...

A mistake hadn't been made
By bringing her home,
Since Vera likes playing
With this little gnome.

Vera chases Emma,
And Emma chases V.
It's really cute!
Oh, you should see.

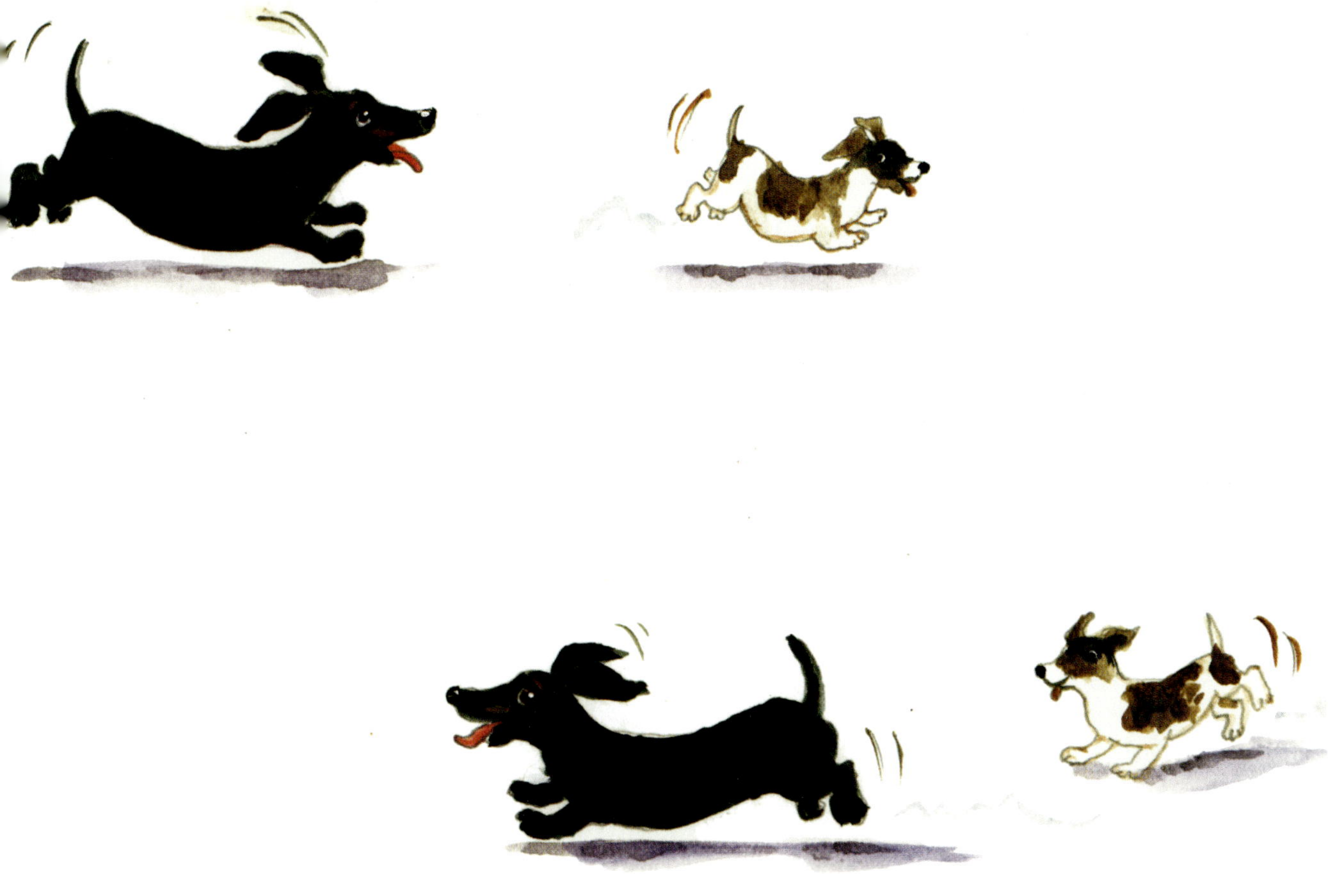

But Buffy still
Has not come around.
A friend in Emma
She has not found.

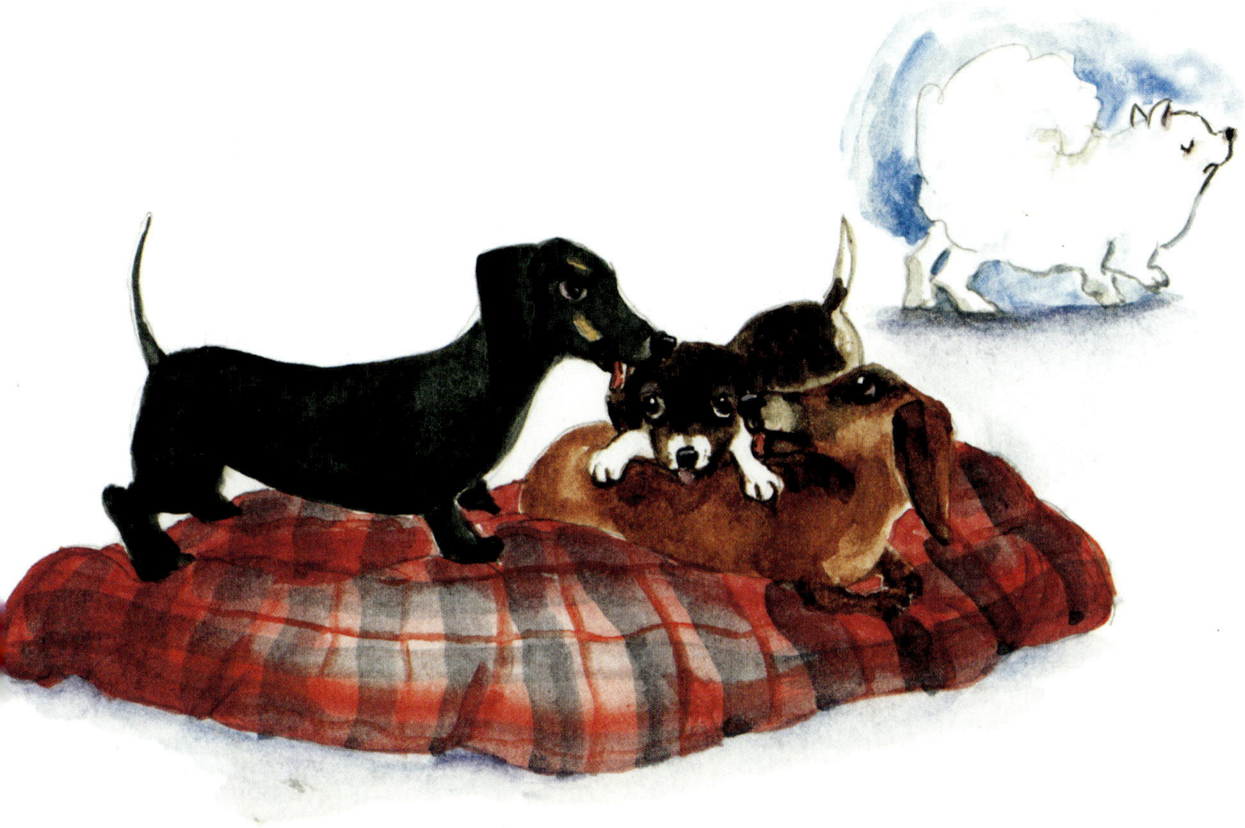

Where Emma is,
There is no Buffy.
I can't figure out
Why she's so stuffy.

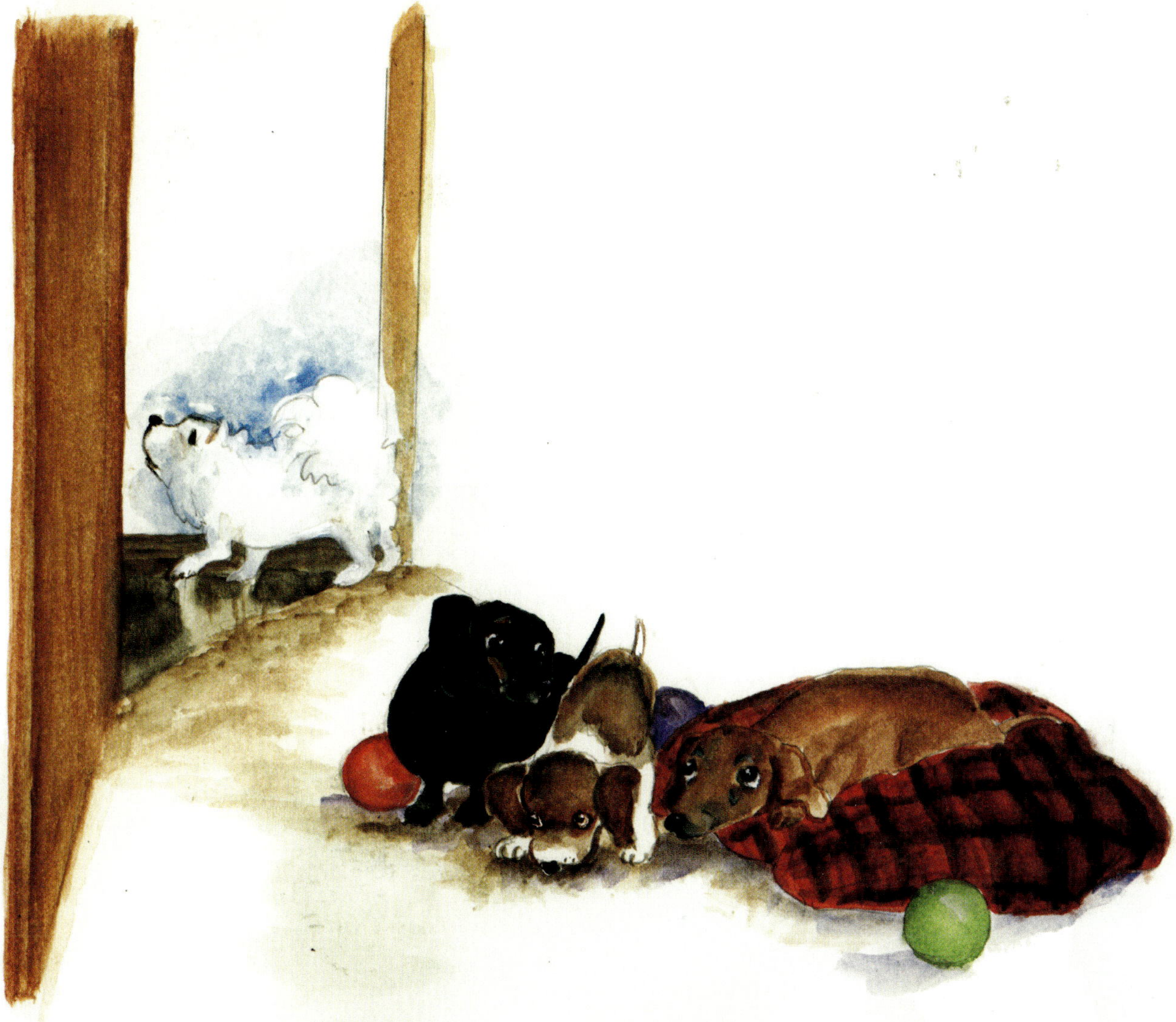

Buffy's anger
Is running deep.
From Emma, she doesn't want
To hear a peep.

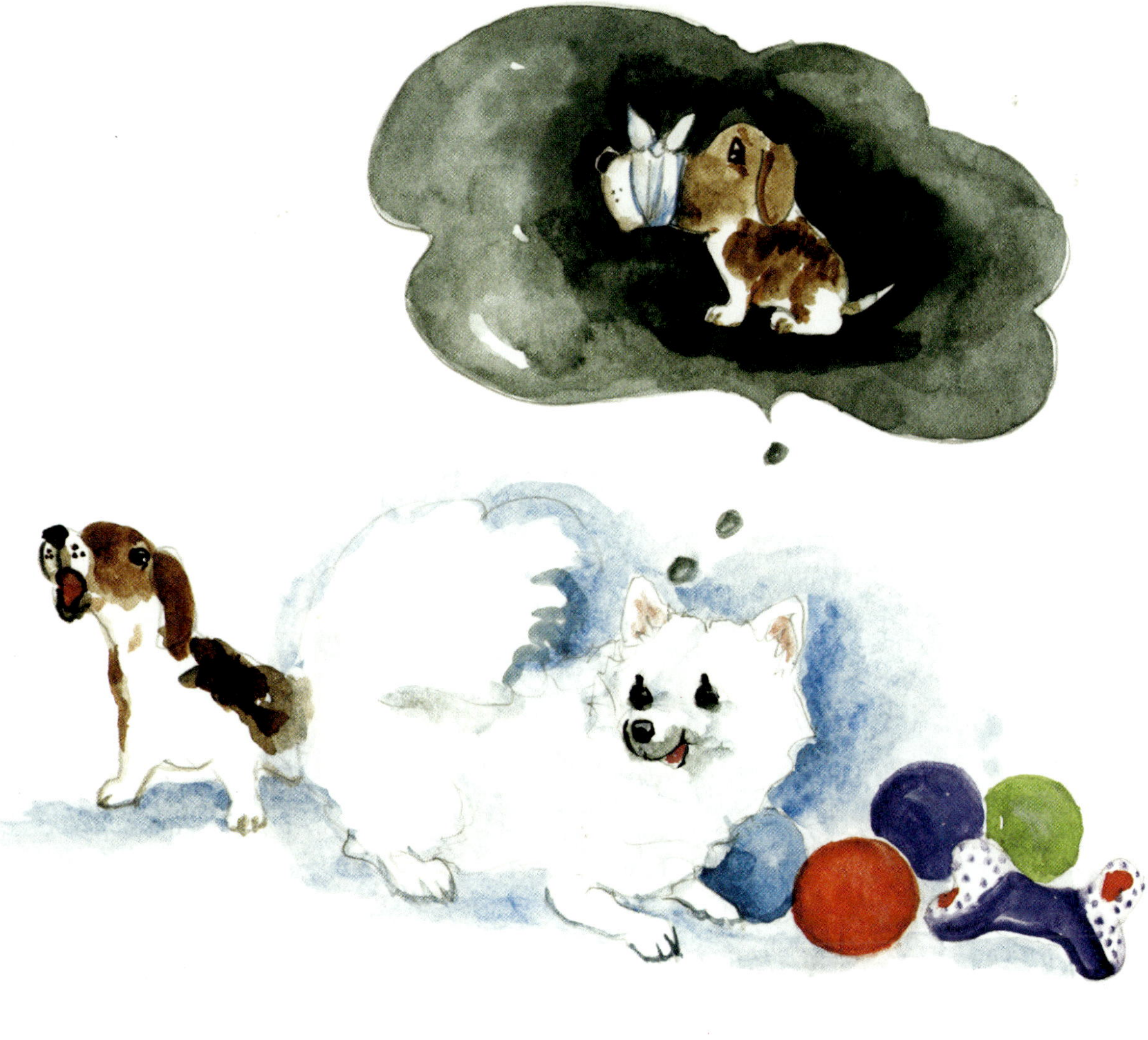

My only hope
Is that, in the end,
Buffy and Emma become
Really great friends.

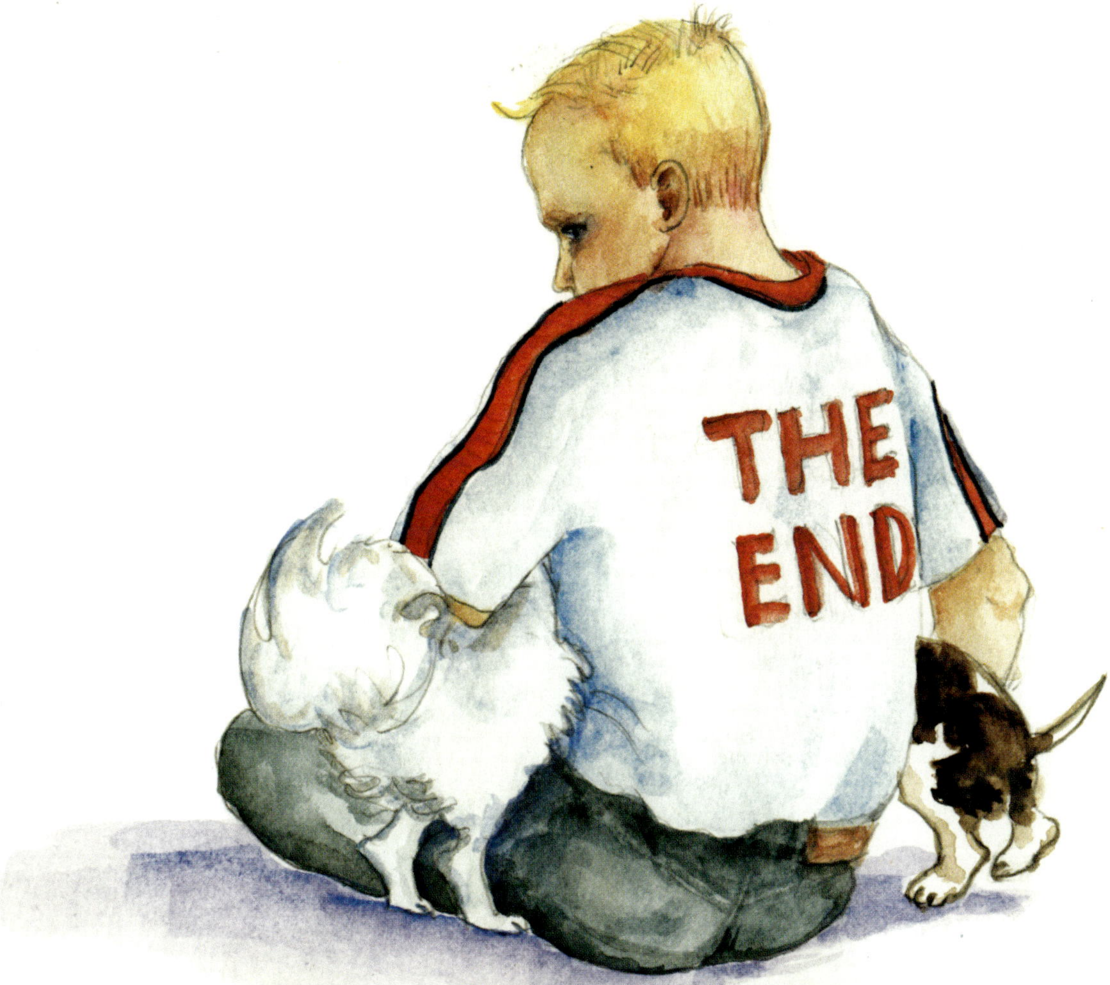
THE
END